DICK KING-SMITH
Mr Ape

Illustrated by
John Eastwood

CORGI YEARLING BOOKS

MR APE
A CORGI YEARLING BOOK : 0 440 86357 0

First published in Great Britain by Doubleday,
a division of Transworld Publishers

PRINTING HISTORY
Doubleday edition published 1998
Corgi Yearling edition published 1999

7 9 10 8 6

Corgi Yearling Books are published by Transworld Publishers,
61–63 Uxbridge Road, London W5 5SA,
a division of The Random House Group Ltd,
in Australia by Random House Australia (Pty) Ltd,
20 Alfred Street, Milsons Point, Sydney, NSW 2061, Australia,
in New Zealand by Random House New Zealand Ltd,
18 Poland Road, Glenfield, Auckland 10, New Zealand
and in South Africa by Random House (Pty) Ltd,
Endulini, 5a Jubilee Road, Parktown 2193, South Africa.

Made and printed in Great Britain by Cox & Wyman Ltd, Reading, Berkshire

Contents

Chapter 1

Ape Has a Brainwave

For some time now, Archibald Peregrine Edmund Spring-Russell of Penny Royal had slept in his kitchen.

It was not on account of a shortage of bedrooms. In fact there were fifteen bedrooms in Penny Royal, a huge rambling barracks of a house, given to an earlier Spring-Russell by King Charles II, for services rendered.

The reason was a simple one. The kitchen was enormous, the kitchen was warm, the kitchen was where Archibald cooked and ate and spent most of his indoor time, so he thought, why not sleep there? And he moved his bed down.

Archibald Spring-Russell lived quite alone at Penny Royal, and the few people who came to the house – the postman, the milkman, the coal-man, the man who came to read the meter – addressed him as 'Mr Spring-Russell'. Not that he ever said much to any of them – he was a man of few words. Some people thought him grumpy, but in fact his manner was really due to shyness. Had any of his old friends (of whom he hadn't many) come to visit (which they didn't), they would not have used the name Archibald, nor Archie, nor either of his other names. They would have called him by the nickname he had acquired as a schoolboy, when, on account of his initials, he had always been known as 'Ape'.

Strangely, this had fitted him. He had been a large, shambling, loose-limbed boy, and now he was a large, shambling, loose-limbed old man, who walked about with long arms hanging low, as though at any moment he might drop onto all fours.

Ape lived alone at Penny Royal for the simple reason that his family had left him. His children (in whom he had never been very interested) had grown up and gone out into the world, and when the last one left, his wife had said, 'Right, Ape, I'm sick of this ugly great house and I'm tired of you, so I'm off.'

For most people this would have been up-setting after thirty years of marriage. But though at first surprised by it, Ape found that he was really rather relieved.

At last he had the place to himself (for his wife, before leaving, had dismissed all the servants), and he thought, I can do as I like. For Mrs Spring-Russell was a very bossy lady, and over the last thirty years Ape had done as he was told.

One of the things he had been told was that no animal of any kind might be kept at Penny Royal. His wife had considered them dirty, and his children, when young, had never been the least bit interested in keeping pets. Whereas Ape as a boy had kept chickens and rabbits and guinea-pigs, and had lavished upon them rather more affection than he had later been able to feel for his sons and daughters, with whom he had little in common.

For one thing, they hadn't much of a sense of humour. Once he had said to them, 'Do you know what you are?'

'No,' they said. 'What?'

'You,' said Ape, 'are the Offspring-Russells,' but they all looked quite blank.

Nor were they particularly nice – quite horrid in fact, selfish and uncaring and rude to the servants.

For the first week or so after the departure of his wife and all the servants Ape made a vague effort to keep the great house clean and tidy, but this, he soon realized, was too much for an old man to do, even a strong old man, and he decided to shut most of the place up.

First he shut up fourteen of the fifteen bedrooms. Then he closed the doors of the huge high-ceilinged drawing room, and the long lofty dining room, and the music room, and the sewing room, and the flower room, and the library, and the billiard room, and the butler's pantry.

Then Ape shut up each of the dozens of other rooms in Penny Royal, except for one bathroom, one lavatory and the kitchen. A couple of weeks later, finding that he spent a great deal of his time in this last-named room, he was able to shut the door of the fifteenth bedroom after spending a day moving his four-poster bed to the kitchen. He took it all to pieces, manoeuvred it bit by bit down the great curving central staircase of the house, and re-erected it nice and near to the warmth of the big old-fashioned coal-

fired range, where the food had been prepared first for the Spring-Russell family, and later, after they had finished their meals, for the cook and the butler and the parlourmaid and the two housemaids and the boy who cleaned the boots.

After a while Ape found that he was rather enjoying cooking for himself. Before, his wife, in consultation with the cook, had always chosen the menus for the day. But now Ape could make all his favourite meals, things he had liked as a boy — sausages, for example, and Welsh rarebit, and fish-fingers, and rice pudding that he mixed with crumbled-up digestive biscuits and strawberry jam. And eggs — boiled, fried, poached, scrambled. Ape was particularly fond of eggs.

Doing the shopping all by himself was another new experience that was fun, so much so that every day he drove into town in his ancient but well-preserved Rolls-Royce, and spent a lot of time in the supermarket, choosing schoolboy food.

Before long it occurred to him — as he was putting a carton of eggs into his trolley — that here was something he needn't buy now.

He could keep his own hens, to provide his own eggs, at home, at Penny Royal!

He thought excitedly about this that evening, as he sat up eating his supper of turkeyburgers and wavy chips and baked beans, with Instant Whip to follow. Now that he had things properly arranged, it was only his lunch that Ape ate at the big wooden kitchen table. His breakfast, and his supper, he naturally ate in bed.

'I shall buy some hens,' he said (to himself but out loud: it was nice to be able to say things without fear of contradiction from his wife). 'But where shall I keep them?'

Naturally, because of Mrs Spring-Russell's aversion to animals, there was no such thing as a chicken-house at Penny Royal. There were stables (where no horse had been allowed) and kennels (where no dog had set foot), and even a great stone dovecot shaped like a pepperpot (from which no dove had ever flown).

'It would be possible,' said Ape, 'to keep hens in one or other of those. But they would not be very comfortable in such cold draughty places, and then if I let them out in the daytime, there's always the risk of a passing fox. What they will need is somewhere warm and dry and comfortable and safe and roomy. But where?'

When Ape had finished his Instant Whip (caramel-flavoured), he got out of bed and put his supper things in a bowl in the kitchen sink to soak. Then he put on his bedroom slippers and an old dressing gown and went out of the kitchen and along a passage that led to the great central hall of Penny Royal.

Around this he shambled, long arms hanging, deep in thought, passing the closed doors of the various rooms.

He stopped by chance outside the door of the drawing room. Absently he opened it and walked in and looked around at the deep arm-chairs and sofas, at the heavy pieces of furniture, at the rich soft carpets.

On one wall of this large room was a full-length portrait of his wife, dressed in a ballgown of a hideous shade of blue, and looking at her bossiest. Ape stood before it, staring up. 'I,' he said, 'am going to keep some hens and you can't stop me!' and he put out his tongue at the portrait. 'But where shall I keep them?' he said as he turned away.

Then it was that A. P. E. Spring-Russell Esquire of Penny Royal in the county of Gloucestershire raised one of his long arms and smote himself upon the forehead with a shout of joy. 'In here!' he cried. 'It's warm and it's dry and it's comfortable and it's safe and it's roomy. I'll keep my hens in my drawing room!'

Chapter 2

Ape Goes to Market

The first thing to be done, Ape realized, was to get rid of the deep armchairs and sofas, the heavy pieces of furniture, the rich soft carpets, none of which would be of any use to hens. Nor would the grand piano, nor the occasional tables with their ornaments, nor the long velvet curtains, nor the gilt-framed paintings upon the walls.

'I shall sell the lot,' said Ape to his wife's portrait, 'except you. You can jolly well stay up there and keep an eye on my hens.

'Come to think of it,' he went on, 'I might as well sell every stick of furniture in the place. It's no use to me, I've got everything I need in the kitchen.'

So it was that before long there was a great sale of the contents of Penny Royal, to which buyers came from all over the country. They saw no sign of the owner, Mr Spring-Russell, though some of them noticed two things. First, that on the kitchen door there was a large notice that read:

and then that in the drawing room there hung a portrait of Mrs Spring-Russell, with a small notice that read: not for sale.

18

'Tragic!' they said to one another. 'The old chap's shut himself away – can't bear to see his precious belongings sold. But he won't part with the picture of his beloved wife.'

Once all the furniture had gone Ape came out of hiding and walked about all over the house, visiting each room and enjoying its bareness. Last of all he came to the drawing room, empty of everything but the portrait and, beneath it, Mrs Spring-Russell's favourite armchair, a great high-backed ornate thing like a throne.

Ape had instructed the auctioneers to put a second not for sale notice on it. He had always hated it, and hoped that his hens would dislike it too and sit in it and show their feelings in the proper manner. He stumped happily round it, his steps loud on the large expanse of bare floor-boards.

'Now,' he said, 'I can buy my hens. But first I must provide for them.'

So he made several journeys into town in the old Rolls-Royce, loading it with sacks of chicken-food and a metal bin to store it in, and feeding-troughs, and water-fountains, and a great many bags of sawdust.

It was not until the drawing room was all

ready to receive its new occupants – the feeding-troughs and water-fountains filled, the sawdust spread over the floorboards – that Ape realized what was missing. Perches! The birds would need somewhere to perch at night. Later Ape lay in bed eating beefburgers and tomato sauce and worrying about the problem, for on the morrow – which was market day – he had planned to buy his hens.

Suddenly he saw the answer, right in front of his eyes.

21

Suspended from the high ceiling of the kitchen, from where they could be lowered by a system of ropes and pulleys, were several long wooden racks, used in the past by the staff of Penny Royal for drying all the laundry of the house. They were in effect aerial clothes-horses, but it was the work of moments for Ape to convert them into down-to-earth hen-perches.

He lowered them, cut through their supporting ropes, carried them through and set them up in the drawing room, and then went happily back to bed and to sleep.

Ape woke next morning with that thrilling feeling of something very exciting about to happen. He boiled the eggs for his breakfast – the last eggs he would have to buy – and then got back into bed and sat up, dipping soldiers into them.

'What sort of hens will they have for sale, I wonder?' he said. 'And how many shall I get? I can buy as many as I like – the drawing room's plenty big enough. I wonder what colour they will be. I hope they'll lay brown eggs – I like brown eggs.'

And then, as he swallowed his last soldier, another worrying thought suddenly occurred to him.

Nest-boxes! They must have somewhere to lay those eggs – not just drop them anywhere on the floor.

As he dressed in the clothes he always wore, a hairy tweed suit of an old-fashioned cut, and brown boots, he stood in the middle of the kitchen, settling the knot of his old school tie and worrying about this problem of nest-boxes.

Then once again he saw the solution right in front of him. Against the wall stood a tall old kitchen dresser of pale-coloured wood, with, beneath its high shelves, six drawers – drawers that were filled with an army of knives, forks and spoons.

'All I need is one of each,' said Ape, and he collected up all the rest and dumped them in a cupboard.

Then he took out the six drawers and laid them along one wall of the drawing room (just beneath the portrait).

Then he fetched some straw from the stables and, while Mrs Spring-Russell looked down with disapproving eyes, filled the drawer-nest-boxes.

Now all was ready.

Ape put on the old brown curly-brimmed bowler hat that he always wore to go to town, and went out to start up the Rolls-Royce.

No sooner had Ape shambled into the covered part of the market which housed the poultry for sale than he saw exactly what he fancied.

There, in a wire cage, were twelve beautiful big brown hens. There were many other pens of birds for sale – white ones, black ones, spotty ones – but Ape hardly gave them a second glance.

By the time the auctioneer came to sell the hens, Ape, having found an ice-cream van, was licking away at a large cornet – his second – of his favourite flavour, strawberry.

When the bidding began for the dozen brown hens, other farmers and poultry-keepers made their bids by a nod or a wink or a tap of the nose or a pull at an ear lobe.

Ape bid by holding aloft his strawberry cornet, and hold it up he did, time and again, till the price rose so high that all the others dropped out, and the birds were knocked down to him.

'Sold to the gentleman in the, er, brown hat,' said the auctioneer.

'Your name, sir?'

'Spring-Russell,' said Ape.

'Address?'

'Penny Royal.'

A moment later one of the hauliers approached Ape, offering to deliver the hens. 'I'm going your way, sir,' he said.

'Don't need you,' said Ape, 'but I'd be obliged if you'd crate them up and stick them in my car.'

'You never saw anything like it,' said the haulier later to a crowd of his mates in the pub. 'There's this big old guy dressed like I don't know what and he pays the earth for a dozen hens and gets me to put 'em in a couple of crates and stow them on the back seat of his car, which just happens to be a Rolls-Royce Silver Ghost, and you'll never guess what he gives me for a tip.'

'Ten p?' they said.

'A ten-pound note,' said the haulier. 'They don't breed 'em like that any more. Ten quid, just for lifting a couple of crates. You could have knocked me down with a feather.'

It wouldn't even have needed a feather to knock the haulier down if he had seen, some time later, twelve beautiful big brown hens wandering contentedly around the great drawing room at Penny Royal, pecking in the feeding-troughs, sipping from the water-fountains, fluttering up to try out the perches.

To put the seal on Ape's pleasure, one of them almost immediately hopped into a drawer and proceeded to lay a beautiful big brown egg, right under Mrs Spring-Russell's nose.

Chapter 3

Ape Has Visitors

That first egg was followed, early next morning, by several more. Soon after waking in his four-poster in the kitchen, Ape heard, coming from the drawing room, the triumphant cackling which every hen makes after laying, and knew that he now had two for his breakfast.

Later, sitting up in bed eating them, he heard more cackles, and by the time he was dressed and had returned to the drawing room, there were half a dozen more eggs in the drawer nest-boxes. In fact, despite making himself scrambled eggs for lunch and an omelette for his supper, there were still a couple of eggs left over by the end of the day.

'Well done, girls!' said Ape proudly when he

went to say good night to his beautiful big brown hens. 'I can see I shall have a job to keep up with you.'

The last of the daylight, coming in through the tall French windows, showed them dozing now on their clothes-rack perches, muttering sleepily to one another.

So busy had Ape been within the walls of

Penny Royal that he had given no thought to what was happening outside. But when, next day, he happened to look out of the French windows, where normally he would have expected to see a great sweep of beautifully mown lawns, he saw instead what looked like a hayfield.

'Hell's bells!' said Ape. 'Of course, she must have sacked the gardeners as well.'

The grounds of Penny Royal were extensive,

and had needed the attentions of two gardeners and a garden boy, but now, as Ape found when he went out to walk around, the place was like a jungle. Apart from the overgrown lawns, the flower-beds were choked with weeds, as was the kitchen garden, where many of the vegetables had gone to seed. Everything was in a terrible mess.

Ape went back indoors, stopping outside the

French windows of the drawing room to admire his hens within, and made himself a large cup of cocoa. He sat dunking biscuits in it.

Over the years he had made a secret study of the art of dunking – secret because Mrs Spring-Russell strongly objected to the practice. He knew the exact length of time for which a particular variety of biscuit might be immersed before becoming too soggy and thus disintegrating into the cup. Digestives were a two-second dunk, Marie three, Royal Scots four, Rich Tea six, and so on.

Today, as he ate his shortbreads (five seconds),

Ape discussed, with himself, the problem of the overgrown grounds. 'I can't possibly manage it all,' he said. 'That's for sure. All that mowing, weeding, sowing, hoeing, that sort of stuff. I suppose I'll have to get the gardeners back. If they haven't found other jobs.

'On the other hand,' he went on, 'I don't really

want to do that. Does it matter if it's all a bit jungly? There's no-one else to see it but me. Though I must say, it looks a frightful mess.'

When he had finished his cocoa, he went back out into the kitchen garden and pulled some bolted lettuces for his hens. Fetching a stepladder and a length of string, he suspended the green stuff from the great glass chandelier that hung from the centre of the drawing room ceiling.

It was while he was watching the birds pecking happily away at the lettuces that Ape suddenly became aware that someone else was watching him. He turned towards the French windows and saw, staring in at him, the mournful face of a donkey. Round its neck, Ape could see, was a length of old rope with a frayed end to it. The creature, it was plain, had been tethered to a post or peg, and the worn rope had snapped, setting it free.

At that moment Ape heard a loud knocking, and he made his way out of the drawing room, shutting the door carefully behind him, and crossed the hall to the great double front doors of Penny Royal.

'Must be the postman,' he said (for the milkman and the coalman and the man who came to

read the meter always used the tradesmen's entrance), but when he opened the doors, he saw, standing at the top of the broad flight of stone steps that led up from the forecourt, a boy, wearing rather ragged clothes and a worried look.

''Scuse me, mister,' said the boy. 'You haven't seen a donkey, have you?'

33

'Yes,' said Ape. 'On my front lawn. The other side of the house.'

The worried look vanished from the boy's brown face, to be replaced by a broad grin. 'Oh thanks, mister!' he cried. 'She's my donkey, you see. Dada bought her specially for me. She's called Columbine, and she broke her tether, and we searched all over the common where our caravan is and we couldn't find her, so I came on up here.'

'Where's your father then?' said Ape.

'He's looking in the fields on either side of your drive,' said the boy. 'I'll call him,' and he put two fingers in the sides of his mouth and let out the loudest, most piercing whistle imaginable.

'Gosh!' said Ape admiringly. 'I've always wanted to be able to do that.'

'I'll teach you,' said the boy.

'Thanks,' said Ape. 'What's your name, by the way?'

'Jake.'

'Come on then, Jake. Let's go and catch your Columbine,' said Ape, and he shambled down the steps, the boy following.

As they set off, Jake pointed down the drive. 'Here's Dada coming now,' he said.

Ape saw a tall dark-skinned man, with longish black hair like the boy, striding towards him. He looked angry.

'Here, you,' he said loudly. 'Where d'you think you're taking my boy?'

A gypsy, thought Ape, and a bad-tempered gypsy at that.

He looked the tall man in the eye – they were much of a height. 'I'm taking your boy to show him where his donkey is,' he said, 'and I'll tell you something – he's a sight politer than his father,' and he turned his back on the gypsy and walked on.

But when they reached the lawn-turned-hayfield, there was no sign of the donkey.

'Funny,' said Ape. 'She was standing just out here', and he pointed to the French windows, behind which stood several of his hens looking out from the drawing room, while others still pulled at the lettuces hanging from the chandelier. From the wall behind, Mrs Spring-Russell seemed positively to glower at the sight of the strangers looking in.

They found Columbine in the overgrown kitchen garden, eating a very large cabbage. The man took hold of her rope, while the boy Jake scrambled up on to the donkey's grey back. He leaned forward, pulling gently at her long ears, and crooning some sort of song to her in a language Ape could not understand.

'Thank you, mister, thank you very much,' he said, smiling at Ape. Ape smiled back. He'd never had a lot to do with his own children, perhaps because they were, in looks and character, very like his wife. Like her, they had actively disliked animals of all sorts. Whereas this boy obviously loved them.

'Sorry,' said Jake's father abruptly. 'I shouldn't have spoken to you like that, sir. I was worried. I didn't know where Jake had got to.' He put out a hand.

Ape shook it. 'Forget it,' he said. 'What's your name?'

'Hart. Joe Hart.'

'You're gypsies, aren't you?'

'We call ourselves Romanies.'

'You're in a caravan, up on the common, Jake was telling me,' Ape said. 'I've always fancied life in a gypsy caravan, moving around the country-side wherever you like, here today, gone tomorrow, always the open road stretching away before you.'

'I dare say you're more comfortable in a great house like this,' said Joe Hart.

'I'm as snug as a bug in a rug,' said Ape. 'It's the outside that's worrying me — this kitchen garden, the lawns and all the rest of it. It's one big mess.'

There was a short silence, broken only by the noise of the donkey champing cabbage. A look passed between father and son, and then Joe said, 'I could lend a hand for a bit, if you like, sir.'

It's a good strong hand too, thought Ape, and the boy could be useful if I should get some more livestock, which I might. Anyway, he's going to teach me to whistle with two fingers.

'All right,' he said. 'Thanks. We'll try it. I'll pay you a fair hourly rate, and you can bring Columbine with you and she can eat her way through this jungle. Does she pull the caravan?'

'Oh no, sir,' said Joe. 'I've got a horse.'

'A skewbald, he is,' said Jake, 'called Billy.'

'Well, bring him too,' said Ape, 'and look here, Joe, there's no need to call me "sir". My name's Spring-Russell, but I'm always known by my initials, you see. A-P-E. Call me Ape.'

'Couldn't do that,' said Joe. 'Wouldn't seem right.'

'But we could call him Mr Ape, couldn't we, Dada?' said Jake.

'No, no,' said Joe.

'Yes, yes,' said Ape.

Chapter 4

Ape Gets Some Pets

A week later, the view from the French windows of the drawing room was rather different.

Ape stood, his hens clucking contentedly around him, and looked out once again at the broad lawns of Penny Royal.

Joe had spent hours mowing them, and had at last made them look a lot more respectable. Each day Jake and he had brought Columbine the donkey and Billy the horse and turned them into the walled kitchen garden, where they feasted.

'Good job you can't see them in there,' Ape said to his wife's portrait. 'You'd have forty fits.'

Jake came into the drawing room. 'Mr Ape?' he said.

'Yes?'

'Do you like rabbits?'

'To eat, d'you mean?'

'No, to keep as pets.'

'Haven't kept any since I was your age.'

'You could now,' said Jake. 'In the dining room. They'd have lots of space to run about.'

Before Ape could comment on this, they heard a noise somewhere up inside the drawing room chimney. It was a scrabbling noise, as of something falling down. First came a shower of soot with some bits of stick mixed in it, and then into the wide empty grate fell a bird.

'What on earth . . . ?' began Ape.

'It's a jackdaw, Mr Ape,' said Jake. 'A young jackdaw. There must be a nest of them in the top of the chimney and this one's come tumbling all the way down.'

'Catch him,' said Ape, but before the boy could lay hands on the bird, it began to flutter around the floor, much to the surprise and annoyance of Ape's hens, who ganged up and began to set upon this black intruder.

The fledgling jackdaw had not yet properly mastered the art of flying, and things would have gone hard with it had not Jake now been able to grab it. It squawked and pecked at him, but he talked to it and soothed it, and soon it ceased to struggle, regarding them both with bright black eyes.

'What shall I do with him, Mr Ape?' Jake asked.

'Well,' said Ape, 'we can't put him back up the chimney, and we can't let him loose in the world – he can't fly well enough yet. So we'll have to keep him, Jake, if he is a he, which we don't know. He can live in the kitchen with me.'

'He'll make messes everywhere, Mr Ape,' said Jake. 'But you could keep him in the dining room. The rabbits wouldn't mind.'

'Rabbits?' said Ape. 'Oh yes, rabbits . . . I remember, you were saying. Tell you what, Jake. We'd better go shopping.'

The following morning Ape made himself one of his favourite breakfasts, a breakfast quite unlike most people's.

First, he opened a tin of creamed rice, poured it into a bowl, added two big spoonfuls of strawberry jam, crumbled some digestive biscuits into the mixture, and stirred it all up together with a spoon.

Then he hard-boiled three brown eggs from his brown hens, squished them up with a fork, added salt, pepper and a large lump of butter, and stirred that up.

Then he got back into bed and sat up against his pillows, happily eating these strange messes and chewing over the idea of buying himself some rabbits. He clearly remembered a particular pet rabbit he had had as a small boy, seventy years ago, and how fond of it he had been. He could picture it still, looking out through the wire of its little hutch.

Ape swallowed his last mouthful. 'I suppose,' he said as he got out of bed to put the dishes in the sink, 'that that rabbit would have been happier if he'd had room to stretch his legs. Not much space in a hutch. Still, there'll be masses in the dining room. In fact I'd better get several rabbits – for company, you know.'

Ape continued talking to himself as he dressed. 'I'll drive into town today,' he said, 'and have a look round the pet shop and see what they've got. Perhaps Jake would like to come with me. I'll ask Joe if he can.'

He found Joe in the stable yard, cleaning the Rolls-Royce. 'Where's Jake?' he asked.

'Looking at Columbine, I expect,' said Joe. 'He fusses about her like nobody's business.'

'Why?' said Ape. 'She's not ill, is she?'

'No,' said Joe. 'She's in foal. Six months gone, so only another three to wait.'

'Gosh!' said Ape. 'Going to have a baby, eh?

How wizard! I'd love to see a baby donkey born here at Penny Royal. I do hope you won't have gone before then – I know you people are always on the move. How long do you plan to stay on the common?'

'We shan't go yet awhile, I hope, Mr Ape,' said Joe. 'Jake here has got a place at the village school, and the term starts soon.'

Ape looked round to see Jake approaching. 'I suppose you've had to go to quite a few different schools, eh?' he said to the boy.

Jake nodded. 'I wish I could stay at the same one like other children do,' he said. 'But as soon as I've made some friends, we move on again.'

'The trouble is the same it's always been,' said Joe Hart. 'People don't feel comfortable with Romany folk. To them we're foreigners at best, selling clothes-pegs and sprigs of lucky heather, eating hedgehogs baked in a clay oven. At worst they think of us as a pack of dirty thieves and try their best to get us shifted somewhere else. We ought to be all right where we are now – it is common land – but sooner or later someone will find a way to get rid of us. It isn't so much that we want to keep moving on – it's that we have to.'

'Couldn't you buy a piece of land?' said Ape. 'They couldn't put you off it then.'

'Land costs money,' said Joe. 'Which I haven't got.'

I have, thought Ape. More than I know what to do with.

Joe gave the windscreen of the Rolls a final going-over with a chamois-leather and stood back to admire his handiwork.

'She hasn't been so clean for donkey's years,' said Ape. 'Which reminds me – I'm going into town this morning. I'm thinking of buying some rabbits.'

'Rabbits?' said Joe. 'To eat, you mean?'

'No, I don't want to eat them,' said Ape. He laughed. 'Though I am going to keep them in the dining room,' he added. 'Now, would it be all right if Jake came with me? He might like a ride in the Rolls, and I'm sure he'd be a help to me in choosing these rabbits. He's good with animals.'

'That's fine by me, Mr Ape,' said Joe. 'I know you'll take good care of him.'

The road to town crossed the common, and as they drove over it the Harts' caravan came into sight, a big old fashioned horse-drawn caravan, brightly painted in red and blue.

Ape slowed and stopped. 'Jake,' he said, 'd'you think I could have a look inside your home? It looks so nice.'

''Course you can, Mr Ape,' said Jake, and they got out of the Rolls and walked across the grass towards the caravan.

'Aren't you afraid someone might steal from it?' Ape asked. 'Now that you and your father are down at Penny Royal all day?'

'No,' said Jake. 'Swift wouldn't let them.'

'Who's Swift?' Ape asked.

For answer Jake put his fingers in the corners of his mouth and out came that piercing whistle. Out too, from under the steps that led up to the back door of the caravan, came a long-legged snake-headed, biscuit-brindled dog, a typical gypsy's lurcher, and ran to Jake and licked his hand, whip tail wagging.

'She's going to have puppies, Mr Ape,' Jake said.

'Wow!' said Ape. 'Your donkey's in foal and your dog's in whelp. Aren't you lucky!'

Inside the caravan, Ape noted immediately how neat and colourful it was, with bright paint and burnished brasswork and lots of gleaming ornaments. There wasn't a speck of dust to be seen, and anyone else would have thought this the home of a very house-proud woman – or, rather, caravan-proud.

But Ape knew, because Joe had told him, that no woman lived here. Joe's wife had died when Jake was small, and the gypsy had brought up his son alone.

As though he had read Ape's thoughts, Jake pointed to a large coloured photograph in a gilded frame that hung upon the wall. It was of a raven-haired woman – not much more than a girl, Ape thought – who stared unsmilingly at the camera. Her face, with its high cheekbones and large dark eyes, was beautiful.

'That's my mum,' Jake said. 'She died.'

Ape nodded. 'Your father told me,' he said.

He thought of adding, 'How very sad' or 'I'm so sorry' or 'You must miss her', but something decided him to say no more. Poor little chap, he thought.

Once again Jake seemed to know what he was thinking. 'It's all right,' he said, as though Ape was the one who needed comforting. 'She died when I was very young. I can't really remember her.'

When they arrived in town, Ape and Jake went first to the bank, where Ape drew out some money, and then on to the pet shop. They made a strangely assorted pair: Ape in his hairy tweed suit, brown boots and brown bowler hat, Jake in old jeans and a T-shirt and trainers, the tall old man lumbering along in his usual way, the boy positively skipping in his excitement.

'How many rabbits are you going to buy, Mr Ape?' he asked as they walked along the high street.

'Depends what they've got,' said Ape.

In fact there were four rabbits for sale in the pet shop, a black one, a grey one, a spotty one and a white one with pink eyes.

'What d'you think, Jake?' said Ape.

'They're all lovely, aren't they?'

'Well, we'll have the lot then.'

'But, Mr Ape,' said Jake, 'hadn't you better ask whether they're bucks or does? Bucks might fight when they're put together.'

'You're right,' said Ape, and he asked the shop-keeper.

'The white one's a buck,' the man said. 'The other three are females.'

'Well,' said Ape again, 'we'll have the lot then.'

'But, Mr Ape,' said Jake again, 'you'll have to keep the buck separate or else you'll have dozens of rabbits before long.'

'Good,' said Ape.

His eye fell upon two large cages full of guinea-pigs. 'Look at those, Jake,' he said. 'I used to keep some when I was your age. I like guinea-pigs – they make nice noises, talking to you all the time,' and to the shopkeeper he said, 'All right to keep rabbits and guinea-pigs together, is it?'

'If you've got plenty of space.'

'I have,' said Ape.

'How many did you want?'

'How many have you got?'

The shopkeeper counted the guinea-pigs. They were of many different colours, some with smooth coats, some with rough, some long-haired. 'There are twelve here altogether to choose from,' he said. 'Was it boars or sows you wanted?'

'Don't mind,' Ape said.

'How many would you like?' asked the man and, for the third time, Ape said, 'We'll have the lot.'

'But, Mr Ape,' said Jake for the third time,

while the man was putting the animals into boxes, 'you haven't asked him how much the rabbits and the guinea-pigs are. Surely you want to know.'

'I'm not bothered,' said Ape.

'How will you manage, sir?' the man asked, looking at the sixteen cardboard carrying-boxes.

'We'll stick 'em in the car,' said Ape. 'Back in five minutes,' and in five minutes' time the owner of the pet shop, for the first and only time in his life, found himself loading four rabbits and twelve guinea-pigs into a Rolls-Royce Silver Ghost.

Back home at Penny Royal, Joe helped to carry the boxes in. On Ape's instructions he had already spread a good layer of sawdust all over the dining-room floor and put food ready, and now the three of them stood and watched as the rabbits hopped, silently, and the guinea-pigs ran, squeaking, about the place. Despite Columbine's best efforts there were still masses of vegetables in the kitchen garden, and soon the new arrivals settled down to feast on a heap of cabbage and carrots. The jackdaw was already much stronger and greeted them with loud squawks.

'Lovely, aren't they, Joe, don't you think?' said Ape.

The gypsy shook his head, smiling. 'Hens in your drawing room, now rabbits and guinea-pigs and a jackdaw in your dining room! Whatever next, Mr Ape?'

'To tell the truth, Joe,' said Ape, 'I'm thinking about using the music room next. It would be the proper place, it seems to me.'

'The music room? What for?'

'You heard them in the pet shop, didn't you, Jake?' said Ape. 'Singing beautifully, they were. I always fancied keeping some canaries.'

Chapter 5

Ape Has a Birthday

Ape and Joe and Jake stood in the music room, looking around. It was a small room by the standards of Penny Royal, at one corner of the house. Thus it had two large windows, one at each side of the right angle, and was very light.

'Why's it called the music room, Mr Ape?' Jake asked. 'Was there a piano in here?'

'No,' said Ape. 'The piano was in the drawing room.'

'Oh,' said Jake. 'Well, if they made music in the drawing room, what did they do in the music room — draw?'

Ape laughed. 'Actually,' he said, 'my wife fancied herself as a harpist. She used to play her harp in here.'

'Like the angels do, in Heaven?'

'Don't know about that,' said Ape. 'I thought she made a devilish noise. Canaries will sound much sweeter.'

Joe looked round the bare room. 'They'll need somewhere to perch, Mr Ape,' he said.

'So they will. Pity that old harp's gone. We could have rigged it up on its side and then they could have perched on the strings.'

'Begging your pardon, Mr Ape,' said Joe, 'but that would never have done. My father always had a canary in his caravan, and I remember him telling me about perches. People give them much too narrow ones, he said, no thicker than a pencil, and that leads to cramp and sore feet and sometimes even broken joints. A canary's perch, he said, must never be less than a centimetre wide.'

'Let's go up into the attics,' Ape said, 'and see what we can find. When I sold the contents of the house, I never bothered with all the junk that's up there.'

In the attics Jake's sharp eyes caught sight of something in amongst the rolls of old carpet and oddments of furniture. It was a bag of golf-clubs, and stencilled on the pocket were the initials

'A.P.E.S-R.' A narrow old-fashioned bag it was, and in it was a set of nine wooden-shafted clubs.

'These would do for perches, wouldn't they, Mr Ape?' Jake said.

'Golly whiskers!' cried Ape. 'My first clubs that I had when I was a boy!'

He pulled them out one by one, naming them as he did so by the old names by which they had been known in his young days: 'Driver, brassie, baffy, mid–iron, mashie, mashie-niblick, jigger, niblick and putter,' he said.

He gauged the width of a shaft between finger and thumb. 'One centimetre!' he said.

So it was that by the time, that afternoon, that Ape and Jake returned from a second expedition to the pet shop, Joe had the music room ready.

He had fixed several lengths of strong twine across the room from one picture-rail to the opposite one. From these each of the golf-clubs was suspended by a long string fastened to either end of it, like a trapeze. Each club had been hung at a slightly different height, and each made a perfect perch for the six canaries which Ape had bought.

Ferreting about in the attics, Joe had found a box full of old kitchen junk and had taken from it saucers and bowls – for seed and for water. He had also filled an empty biscuit-tin to act as a bath – 'I remember,' he said, 'that father's canaries used to love to have a bath.'

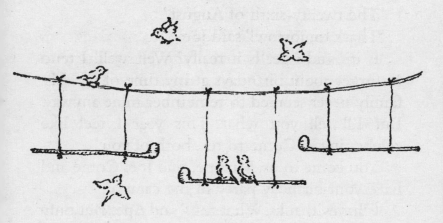

Round and round the music room the six birds flew, chirruping to each other with joy at this newfound freedom, and before long two of them actually pitched on one of the golf-clubs (the putter, it was). They perched there, side by side, their little feet gripping the hickory shaft comfortably. Their combined weight, tiny though it was, was just enough to set the trapeze swinging gently.

'Perfect!' said Ape. 'Wizard idea of yours, Jake; and Joe, you've fixed it all up beautifully. Fancy those old clubs coming in so useful. I was given them for my twelfth birthday, I remember.'

'When is your birthday, Mr Ape?' asked Jake.

'The twenty-sixth of August.'

'That's tomorrow!' said Joe.

'Is it?' said Ape. 'Is it really? Well, well! I tend to forget about birthdays at my time of life. My family never seemed to remember mine anyway. But I'll tell you what. This year I feel like celebrating it. Come to tea, both of you.'

'You come to us, Mr Ape,' said Joe. 'Come and have your birthday party in the caravan.'

'Oh, yes, thanks. What fun!' said Ape. 'But only if you'll let me bring all the grub.'

Early next morning Ape went to the door in dressing gown and slippers to answer the postman's knock.

'Morning, Mr Spring-Russell,' the postman said. 'And a beautiful morning it is too.'

'It is, by Jove!' said Ape.

He did not say it was his birthday, though later he did examine the post more carefully than usual. But no-one had sent him so much as a

card. However, it seemed to him that his canaries were singing even more tunefully than ever in the music room, that in the dining room his rabbits were hopping more happily, his guinea-pigs chattering more cheerfully and the jackdaw squawking more raucously, and what's more, as though to celebrate the occasion, every single one of his twelve hens in the drawing room had already laid him a beautiful brown birthday egg.

After scrambling some for his breakfast in bed, he dressed in his usual clothes, and drove into town in the Rolls to buy what he needed for the party.

'There ought to be a birthday cake, I suppose,' he said as he drove along (never exceeding thirty m.p.h. – he did not approve of speeding). 'But I shan't bother with candles – I'd need too many. And I'll jolly well have my favourite sort – a great big lardy-cake, all lovely and greasy and full of sultanas and currants.'

Once in the supermarket, Ape filled his trolley with exactly the things that small children like best (because they happened to be the things he liked best too).

To drink, he bought Coke and 7-Up and Lilt, and to eat, he bought Jammy Dodgers and Wagon Wheels and Penguins and Jaffa Cakes and Twix and Chocolate Fingers, and, of course, the lardy-cake.

At teatime Ape drove the Rolls up to the common and they all carried the food into the caravan.

Inside, Ape heard little squeaking noises coming from the basket in which Swift was lying. He looked at Joe and Jake, his eyebrows raised questioningly.

'Yes,' said Joe. 'She whelped this morning.'

'Look, Mr Ape,' said Jake, and there beside the lurcher bitch were four tiny puppies.

When at last he could eat no more, Ape sat back and patted his tummy. 'That was good!' he said.

He saw Joe look at Jake and nod, and then Jake said, 'We've got a present for you, Mr Ape, but you can't have it yet.'

'Oh lawks!' said Ape. 'I didn't expect a present.'

'You'll have to wait a good few weeks,' said Joe.

Ape frowned, puzzled.

'It has to stay with its mother for now,' said Jake.

The penny dropped. Ape's frown turned into a huge grin and he pointed at the basket in the corner of the caravan. 'D'you mean . . . ?' he began.

'We'd like you to have the pick of the litter, Mr Ape,' said Joe.

Chapter 6

Ape Gets Nice Surprises

That night Ape found it hard to get to sleep in the big four-poster bed in the kitchen. He was so excited.

When young, he had never had a dog of his own, and once Mrs Spring-Russell came on the scene, there was no chance of his having one. Now – or at any rate in a couple of weeks – he would be the proud owner of the pick of Swift's litter!

'I wonder which one I'll choose,' he said. 'And what shall I call it? Depends whether I have a dog or a bitch, I suppose. Which shall I have? By Jove, what fun it all is!'

When at last he stopped talking to himself, his last thought before he fell asleep was that of all his seventy-five birthdays, this one had been the nicest.

Ten days or so later, something else happened that took his mind off the puppies.

It was Jake who noticed it first. Because he was so good with the animals, Ape let him help with the care of the hens, and the rabbits and guinea-pigs, and the canaries.

One morning a few days before he was due to start at the village school, Jake came out of the dining room and ran across the hall and down the passage to the kitchen. 'Mr Ape! Mr Ape!' he called excitedly. 'The spotty one's plucking!'

Ape turned round from the sink, where he was washing up the breakfast things (he'd had fish-fingers and baked beans and cheese-and-onion flavoured crisps, a mixture of which he was very fond). 'Plucking?' he said. 'Spotty one? What on earth are you talking about, Jake?'

'The rabbit!' Jake said. 'The spotty doe. She's plucking the fur from under her chin and off her chest, to make a nest. She's going to have babies soon.'

'Golly whiskers!' said Ape. 'She would be, wouldn't she? They must have been here nearly a month now.'

'You'll have to move her, Mr Ape,' said Jake, 'and the other two does as well. They can't stay in there with the buck and all the guinea-pigs and the jackdaw, and anyway there's nowhere for them to make their nests. They can't just have their babies in the middle of the dining-room floor. Where can we put them?'

Ape thought. 'Got it!' he said. 'In the butler's pantry. That's the place! Not too big, nice and snug, and there's a row of cupboards all along one wall at floor level – where the silver was kept. Open the doors of those, and they can each choose one.'

'They'll need some stuff to make their nests with,' said Jake. 'As well as their own fur, I mean. Some nice soft hay.'

'Of course, of course,' said Ape. 'Come on, let's move them straight away.'

So they did.

In the butler's pantry the three does, the spotty, the grey and the black, hopped curiously about, noses working, and before long the spotty doe picked up a mouthful of hay and carried it into one of the open cupboards.

'We shall have lots of rabbits soon, shan't we, Mr Ape?' said Jake.

'Yes,' said Ape, 'and lots of guinea-pigs too. I suppose we'd better start thinking about them.'

'No hurry,' said Jake. 'Rabbits take thirty-one days to have babies, but I expect you remember that guinea-pigs take more like seventy. Because their babies are born with their fur on and their eyes open and they start eating almost straight away. We needn't worry about the guinea-pigs yet.'

'Of course,' said Ape. 'I remember now. Gosh, Jake, I don't know what I'd do without you.'

A couple of days later the rabbit population of Penny Royal trebled, as the spotty doe gave birth to eight babies in the butler's pantry, and by then both the black and the grey doe had each chosen a cupboard and were plucking.

All this excitement kept Ape from going to see the puppies, and then, just when he had determined he would go up to the common the very next day, something else happened.

It had become the custom for Joe and Jake, at the end of each working day, to come into the kitchen for tea and biscuits.

'Well, Jake,' said Ape as he dunked a biscuit (Rich Tea – six seconds), 'it's a special day for you tomorrow, eh? Starting school, aren't you?'

Jake nodded.

'It might be a special day for someone else too, Mr Ape,' said Joe.

'Who?'

'Columbine. Looks like she might foal tonight. If it's all right by you, I'll bring her into the stables, and Jake and I will stay with her. She might need help.'

'Of course, of course,' said Ape. 'I'll come down later to see how it's going.'

When Ape came back again, he found that Joe had bedded Columbine down in a loose-box. 'Anything happening?' he asked.

'She'll be a while yet, Mr Ape,' said the gypsy.

'I'll wait up with you.'

'No need. I'll come and tell you when she foals.'

'No, no, I wouldn't miss this for the world,' said Ape. 'Tell you what, I'll go and make us a thermos of cocoa and some sandwiches. Spam all right?'

The cocoa drunk, the sandwiches eaten, the three of them sat side by side on a bale of straw, their backs against the wall, waiting and watching.

Try as he would, Jake could not keep his eyes open. He fell asleep leaning against his father. The hours passed, and the old man, like the boy, could not stay awake and his chin dropped upon his chest. When he woke again, it was to see Joe and Jake kneeling beside something that lay in the bedding of the box, something small and blackish and wet that was making little snorting gasping noises as its mother licked it.

As Ape levered himself to his feet, the gypsy looked up, smiling. 'A filly foal!' he said.

Awkwardly, for his old joints were stiff, Ape lowered himself to his knees beside the newborn child. 'Shall you keep her, Joe?' he asked softly.

'No, Mr Ape. When she's old enough, I shall sell her.'

'To me?'

'If you like.'

Chapter 7

Ape Does a Deal

Not until the donkey foal had managed – after several unsuccessful attempts – to get to its feet could Ape drag himself away from the sight of this new arrival at Penny Royal, so that dawn was breaking as he walked up from the stables to the house.

As he crossed the hall on his way to the kitchen, a hen in the drawing room announced the laying of an early egg, while in the music room a canary sang its first song of the day. Hearing his footsteps on the great tiled floor of the hall, all the guinea-pigs in the dining room began a squealing that said plainly, 'Bring us breakfast!' but Ape was too tired to do more than take off his jacket and pull off his

boots before dropping onto his bed.

It was past eleven when he woke again, he saw by the kitchen clock, and his first thought was that he had fed none of his animals. 'Ah, but Jake will have seen to them all!' he said with relief.

Only then did he remember that Jake was now at school.

When at last he had tended to his livestock (increased yet again, for the grey doe had produced six babies in the butler's pantry), Ape set about getting himself some lunchtime breakfast. Because it was so late, he did not have it in bed but sat at the kitchen table, eating rice crispies and squashed-up banana and raspberry yoghurt, all stirred together.

'How I shall miss that boy when the Harts move on,' he said with his mouth full. 'I hadn't realized how much he has to do each day; and now there'll be more to do – another lot of little rabbits from the black doe soon, and masses of baby guinea-pigs before long. At least the hens can't produce anything because I haven't got a cockerel, but the canaries probably will. And before you can say Jack Robinson, the puppy will be here. And, of course, there's the baby donkey – I must be sure and give Joe a good price for her when the time comes. Don't know what I'll do without him either. Still, thank goodness Jake *has* gone to school – that should keep them here.'

Later that afternoon Ape was standing in the loose-box, feeding an apple to Columbine and telling her how beautiful her daughter was, when Joe and Jake came in.

'I took a few hours off to get some sleep, Mr Ape,' Joe said. 'After I'd seen to Billy.'

'Quite right,' said Ape. 'What d'you think of the foal, Jake?'

'She's beautiful,' said Jake.

'Just what I was telling Columbine. How did you like your first day at a new school?'

'It was all right, Mr Ape,' Jake said.

'He got into a fight,' said his father, 'with one of the big boys.'

'Really?' said Ape. He took Jake by the shoulders and turned him round to look at him. 'Can't see any cuts or bruises,' he said.

'No,' said Joe, 'but the other boy's got a lovely black eye, a proper shiner.'

'He called me names, Mr Ape,' said Jake.

'What like?'

'He said we were dirty gyppos.'

'I bet he won't say that again in a hurry,' said Ape.

Quietly, while the boy was talking to the donkey, Joe said to Ape, 'It's the best thing that could have happened really. They're a nice lot of kids at that school – there's just this one that's a bit of a bully. I don't think he'll mess with Jake any more. The headteacher was very good about it all, pleased in fact, if you ask me. This other boy has quite a name for throwing his weight about.'

'Talking of names,' said Ape, 'what are we going to call this foal, Jake?'

Jake smiled.

'I don't really know. I'm so glad I'll be able to watch her grow up.'

If, thought Ape, you and your father don't move on, as gypsies will, and he suddenly realized with a pang of sadness how lonely he would be when they did. 'Of course, of course,' he said gruffly. 'Now then, Jake, you choose a name for her. What about a flower? Her mother's called after a flower. Have you got a favourite one?'

Jake thought for a bit, frowning with the effort. Then he said, 'Hollyhock.'

'Perfect!' said Ape. 'Hollyhock she is. And by the way, she's not the only new arrival. The grey rabbit's had six. Come and have a look.'

But when Ape and Jake entered the butler's pantry, they found that the rabbit population of Penny Royal was now two dozen. Within the last few hours the black doe had also given birth to six babies.

'That reminds me, we shall need more rabbit food before long, Mr Ape,' Jake said, 'and canary seed.'

'Let's go and have a check-up,' said Ape.

Together they walked across the hall to the first of two smaller rooms that were now used as stores.

In the flower room were kept the bedding materials, sawdust and straw, and also hay. Here too was kept something Jake had found in the attics, a big old-fashioned pram in which, long ago, the young Spring-Russells had been wheeled about the grounds of Penny Royal by their nursemaids. Into this each day Jake loaded all that he needed – the food, the bedding, the sawdust, fresh water in plastic bottles, a broom, a dustpan and brush, a shovel, a bucket – and pushed it round from room to room.

In the sewing room were kept the food supplies, in old biscuit-tins and tea-canisters (also
found in the attics). Only thus were the stocks of
rabbit-mixture and canary-seed safe from other
greedy little mouths. Ape's pets were not the
only creatures in the house: there were a great
many mice.

At either side of these small rooms stood two
large ones, the library and the billiard room.
Each was unchanged from its original use, for
Ape loved his books and his billiards, a game he
had now begun to teach to Jake: the boy was not
yet quite tall enough and had to stand upon an
apple-box to play his shots.

Now, in the sewing room, Jake checked over
the supplies of food as Ape watched. 'I think
we'll last till the weekend,' he said.

'I can pop down to the pet shop any time,' said
Ape. 'Tomorrow, if you like.'

'School,' said Jake.

'What? Oh yes, I get it, you want to come too.
All right, we'll go on Saturday morning.'

On Saturday the owner of the pet shop
rubbed his hands at the sight of Ape. He knew
a good customer when he saw one. 'Good
morning, Mr Spring-Russell!' he said. 'What

76

can we do for you today?'

'My assistant has a list of the stuff we need,' said Ape. 'I'll just have a look round,' and leaving Jake to it, he lumbered off to see what was for sale.

To be fair, Ape had not come with the intention of buying any animals. He had a look at some hamsters (but they were all asleep), and at some pet mice ('But we've already got enough of your sort at home,' he said).

'Home, sweet home,' said a voice. 'Bob's your uncle!'

'I beg your pardon?' said Ape, turning to see who had spoken. There was no-one near – Jake and the shopkeeper were busy at the other end of the shop but otherwise it was empty of people.

'Beg your pardon, grant your grace. Mind the cat don't scratch your face,' said the voice, and then Ape, looking up, saw, in a large cage above his head, a green parrot.

'Bob's your uncle!' it said again.

'By Jove!' said Ape. 'D'you know, I did have an uncle called Bob! I must say, old chap, you talk extremely well.'

'Ding dong bell,' said the parrot. 'Pussy's in the well. Pass the mustard. God save the Queen!'

Ape was fascinated by the clarity of the bird's speech. 'I say!' he called to the shopkeeper. 'Is this parrot for sale?'

The man came over, Jake following. 'Oh yes, Mr Spring-Russell,' he said. 'He's a wonderful talker, he is. He doesn't make a lot of sense but he's very quick at copying things, aren't you, you silly old chap.'

'Silly old chap,' said the parrot.

'How much d'you want for him?' said Ape.

'I'm afraid,' said the shopkeeper, 'that a bird like that is very expensive.'

'How much?' said Ape and, at the figure the man mentioned, the parrot gave a long low whistle.

'What do you think?' Ape asked the bird.

'Bob's your uncle,' said the parrot.

'Chuck in the cage and a packet of parrot food,' said Ape, 'and it's a deal.'

'A cage like that is very expensive, you know.'

'Take it or leave it.'

'All right then, Mr Spring-Russell,' said the shopkeeper. 'Seeing as you're such a good customer. Mind you, I think you've got a bargain.'

'A bargain,' said the parrot.

Chapter 8

Ape Gets Some Advice

O ne evening some weeks later the gypsy and his son sat side by side on the steps of their caravan, enjoying the dusk of an unusually warm October evening. On the grass below them the lurcher bitch Swift lay upon her side, all her pups now gone. Once Ape had taken his pick of the litter, Joe had had no trouble in selling the rest. There were plenty of local sportsmen who knew the potential worth of such gypsy dogs, so fleet of foot, so quick to pick up rabbit or even hare on a dark night, very likely on someone else's land.

All the pups, a dog and three bitches, had been brindled like the mother. Ape had picked the dog puppy, a week ago now.

As they sat and watched the moon swim up over the rim of the common, Jake said, 'I'm worried about Mr Ape, Dada.'

'Worried? Why?'

'Because the way he's going on, I think he's going to fill every room in that great big house with animals, and then how will he manage when we move on? He's finally released the jackdaw back into the wild, but next time we go to the pet shop, he'll probably come back with mice and gerbils and hamsters, and they'll all start breeding, just like the rabbits and the guinea-pigs. There are forty-two guinea-pigs now and the rabbits have got up to twenty-four and he's put the does back with the buck so there'll soon be loads more. Why d'you think he wants so many animals?'

'His wife wouldn't let him keep any,' said Joe. 'He told me. But you're right, Jake, it's all getting out of hand. And I'll tell you another thing . . . he's always talking to himself, but now he's forever chatting away — to the small animals, to the donkey foal, to the puppy, to the parrot (and of course the parrot talks back). It's getting like a madhouse.'

'Mr Ape's not mad, Dada,' said Jake.

'No, I know, he's just a lonely old man. All the same, after what you've said I'll have a chat with him tomorrow, after you've gone to school.'

The next day Joe rode the horse Billy up the long drive to Penny Royal, a drive which had once been kept neat and orderly, fringed by well-tended shrubs and bordered by white-painted iron railings. Now much of the paint had flaked off the rusting rails, the shrubs had grown into a jungle, and the surface of the drive itself was cracked and broken, with weeds sprouting through.

Joe rode across the lawns, still, despite his best efforts, not much more than a rough field, to the kitchen garden.

He called to Columbine, who ambled up, Hollyhock skittering alongside, and put a halter

on her to take her down to water at the stable-
yard trough. He looked about at the ruins of
what had once been the pride of Penny Royal's
head-gardener, with its orderly plots of vegetables, and the fine fruit trees that grew against its
walls, and its greenhouses; these were now
derelict, the donkey had gnawed the bark of
apple, plum and peach trees, and everywhere
there was a wild tangle of bolted green stuff.

Later, Joe made his way round to the back door of the house, which led directly into the kitchen. He raised the heavy brass knocker shaped like a fish (the crest of the Spring-Russell family was a leaping salmon) and let it fall.

Before the echoes of the noise had died away, he heard a voice say loudly – in Ape's unmistakable tones – 'Kindly go away! I am extremely busy!'

That's not like the old boy, Joe thought, he's usually so polite. He walked back round the side of the house, only to see Ape coming out of the front door, carrying his puppy. He marched down the steps and put it on the ground, saying firmly, 'Now then, my lad, that's the place to do it – outside. Not in the middle of the hall.'

'Sorry about disturbing you just now,' said Joe.

'Disturbing me?'

'I knocked on the back door and you said to go away, you were very busy.'

Ape gave a roar of laughter. 'That must have been Bob,' he said. 'He's got my voice to a T.'

'The pup looks well,' said Joe. 'What d'you call him?'

'Speedy,' said Ape. 'Because he already is. And he's quick to learn too. That was the first and

only mistake we've had in the house – my fault,
I should have put him out earlier. Come and
have a cup of tea.'

In the kitchen the green parrot sat silent in his
cage.

'I hear you've been a naughty boy, Uncle Bob,'
said Ape.

'Kindly go away!' said Uncle Bob. 'I am
extremely busy!'

'Good imitation, isn't it?' said Ape.

He unlatched the door of the cage and the
parrot emerged slowly, inspecting Joe with a
bright considering eye.

'Can he fly?' asked Joe.

'No,' said Ape. 'He's grounded. His flight
feathers on one wing have been clipped.'

'Silly old chap,' said Uncle
Bob in an ordinary
parrot voice, as he
walked up Ape's
sleeve and sat
upon his
shoulder.

'He's handsome,' said Joe.

'Handsome is as handsome does,' said the parrot, and he raised his tail and made a mess on the floor. 'Bob's your uncle!' he cried triumphantly.

'I'm afraid his house-training isn't going as well as Speedy's,' said Ape.

'Good boy, Speedy,' said Uncle Bob in Ape's voice, and the brindled pup's whip-tail wagged happily.

When they had drunk their tea, Ape said, 'I haven't collected the eggs today yet. You might like some.'

In the drawing room, while Ape was picking up the eggs, the gypsy caught the eye of Mrs Spring-Russell on the wall. What would she say? he thought. What shall *I* say? How shall I start?

Ape's next words gave him the answer to that: 'Only four today,' he said, straightening up. 'Some of these birds have gone broody, that's the trouble. Now if I only had a cockerel, they could be sitting on fertile eggs and we could have lots and lots of chicks. Perhaps I should buy one. What do you think, Joe?'

Joe took another look at Mrs Spring-Russell and a deep breath. 'No, Mr Ape,' he said. 'Since you ask me, I certainly don't think you should. At least in this room the numbers can't increase, or in the music room where the canaries are all cock birds. Because before long you're going to have a plague of rabbits and guinea-pigs in the dining room, and then you'll be starting to fill the upstairs rooms and where will it all end? It's not really my business, but I think you should be getting rid of animals, not getting more.'

'Get rid of them all?' said Ape. 'Not Speedy?'

'No, of course not.'

'Or Hollyhock?'

'No, of course not.'

'Or Uncle Bob?'

'No, of course not!' shouted the parrot.

'What I mean is,' said Joe, 'why not sell the babies you've bred? All those little rabbits, and then all the little guinea-pigs – there are thirty of those already, Jake said.'

'Thirty-five,' said Ape. 'Another lot last night.'

'There you are, you see. Think of all the children who'd love to have one or two of those as pets.'

'But I don't know any children,' said Ape. 'Except Jake.'

'I do,' said Joe. 'All the kids at his school. They'd have them.'

'I suppose you're right,' said Ape. 'But even if I did that, there'd soon be lots more babies.'

'If you keep both sexes. Why not just keep the doe rabbits and the guinea-pig sows? And don't buy a cockerel.'

'And Bob's your uncle,' said the parrot.

Chapter 9

Ape Starts a Fire

For the rest of that week Ape considered Joe's advice. At the weekend he consulted Jake. They were playing a game of billiards at the time, and Jake, standing on his apple-box, was lining up a long pot on the red.

'Jake!' said Ape suddenly just as the boy was playing the shot.

'Mr Ape!' said Jake. 'You put me off!'

'Sorry,' said Ape. 'I was just going to ask you to do me a favour.'

'What sort of a favour?'

'Well, you see . . .' began Ape, and then he outlined the plan on which he had decided.

'If I write it all out,' he said, 'could you take the notice to your headmaster and see if it's OK by him?'

Jake nodded.

'Thanks,' said Ape. 'Look, have that shot again.'

But once more, just as the boy played the pot, Ape's voice rang out saying, 'Jake!'

This time Jake missed the red ball completely. 'Oh honestly, Mr Ape . . . !' he began, but when he turned round, Ape was shaking his head and grinning and pointing to a chair where Uncle Bob was perching.

'Foul stroke,' said the parrot.

Ape gave a lot of thought to the wording of the notice that Jake was to take to school on the Monday. He wanted to be sure that any animal he parted with would be properly looked after, and though he didn't intend to ask any money for it, he thought that getting something for nothing was not a good idea.

So the notice that Jake took (and that the headmaster approved) read as follows:

LETTER-WRITING COMPETITION

RABBITS — GUINEA-PIGS — CANARIES. IF YOU WOULD LIKE ONE OR MORE OF ANY OF THESE ANIMALS, ALL YOU HAVE TO DO IS TO WRITE A LETTER TO MR SPRING-RUSSELL OF PENNYROYAL. THE LETTER MUST EXPLAIN WHAT YOU WANT AND WHY YOU WANT IT AND HOW YOU WILL LOOK AFTER IT.

LETTERS MUST BE ACCOMPANIED BY A NOTE FROM PARENTS GIVING THEIR PERMISSION.

THE WRITERS OF THE BEST LETTERS WILL EACH RECEIVE AS A PRIZE THE ANIMAL OF THEIR CHOICE —FREE.

'There!' said Ape as he finished writing this at the kitchen table. 'What d'you think of that then?' and Jake said, 'Fine,' and Speedy thumped his tail on the floor, and Uncle Bob said, 'Kindly go away! I am extremely busy!'

By the end of October Ape's menagerie had grown very very much smaller. So many children had written, wanting rabbits or guinea-pigs or canaries, and Ape hadn't had the heart to refuse any of them. A surprising number of applicants claimed that Jake Hart was their best friend. Not only the buck rabbit and all the babies had gone but two of the does as well, leaving only the spotty doe. She and two female guinea-pigs (all the rest had been snapped up) had now been moved from the dining room to share the music room with its last remaining inhabitant, a cock canary who sang happily to them from his golf-club swing.

Speedy and Uncle Bob still lived in the kitchen, of course, and the hens in the drawing room, but the animal population of Penny Royal had dwindled to almost nothing.

Ape found that he could not regret this, for he had made a great many children happy. Joe was glad that no more animals of any kind could be born in the house. Jake was not sorry to have less to do – it gave him more time for his homework – and pleased because the parrot seemed to have taken a great fancy to him. Whenever he was in the house, Uncle Bob would follow him around with his rolling sailor's gait, shouting, 'Jake! Jake! Wait for me! Bob's your uncle!'

One morning at the beginning of November Ape said to Joe, 'I'm just on my way into town. It's Guy Fawkes Night this coming Sunday and I thought I'd buy a nice lot of fireworks. Haven't had any for years and years, but I always enjoyed them as a boy. Jake would enjoy it, wouldn't he?'

'He would,' said Joe. 'So would I.'

So Ape went off and had a lovely time buying rockets and Catherine wheels and roman candles and jumping-jacks and sparklers.

As it grew dark on the Sunday evening, everything was ready. Safety was, as always on Guy Fawkes Night, the main thing to be thought of, not just of the people but of the animals. Swift had been left at home in the caravan. Speedy was shut in the kitchen with Uncle Bob. Billy and the donkeys were far enough away to be in no danger, and the hens and the remaining small animals were of course perfectly safe inside the house.

Ape and Joe had built a big bonfire of old bits of wood and other rubbish in the middle of the sweep of gravel before the front door. In the centre of the bonfire was a guy dressed in some of Ape's old clothes (and looking not unlike him).

Once it was dark enough, they set it alight.

Jake stood watching, twirling a sparkler, as the poor old guy burned and fell. Then the two men began to set off the fireworks, and the rockets soared and the Catherine wheels spun and the roman candles flared and the jumping-jacks fizzed and jumped. And all the time the bonfire blazed and the sparks shot upwards into the night sky.

So busy were they all with the fireworks that
no-one noticed when some old, very dry planks
of wood that were in the middle of the bonfire
suddenly collapsed, sending up a pillar of fat
sparks. No-one saw the wind catch one of those
sparks and lift it high on to the roof of Penny

Royal. No-one knew that just at that point of the roof stood the tall chimney stack of the disused drawing room fireplace, nor that in the top of that chimney was wedged a collection of bits of paper and straw and old sticks, the remains of that nest from which the young jackdaw had fallen down the chimney. For hundreds of years jackdaws had nested in the tops of this and the many other chimneys of Penny Royal. But now they never would again.

The single spark fell into this rubbish and set the paper and straw on fire, and then the sticks caught alight and began to burn fiercely. Unknown to all those below, this fireball fell down the drawing room chimney on to the hearth beneath, where, as they blazed up, the flames took hold of the varnished wood of the great mahogany mantelshelf above the fireplace. The terrified hens, woken suddenly from their mumuring slumber, fluttered from their perches and began to run blindly about the huge high-ceilinged room.

Chapter 10

Ape Hits Rock Bottom

Not until the final rocket was lit – a specially big one that Ape had saved till the end – did anyone notice anything.

As he had done with all the other rockets, Ape aimed it well away from the house. But this last one decided to swerve violently in flight and burst right above Penny Royal, sending out a great shower of golden globes.

As the watchers looked at these floating gently earthwards and vanishing one by one, Joe suddenly noticed smoke coming out of one of the chimney stacks. 'Look, Mr Ape!' he called, pointing upwards.

'Blimey O'Reilly!' cried Ape. 'That's the drawing room chimney! Something's on fire!'

'I'll go and have a look through the French windows,' said Joe, and he ran round the side of the house, carrying the garden fork, with which he had been stoking the bonfire.

Ape made for the front door.

By the time Joe reached the French windows of the drawing room, the inside of it was well alight, and in the glare of the flames the frantic hens were fluttering up and down inside the glass.

Hurriedly the gypsy tried the handles of the windows but they were locked on the inside. Quickly, with several strong blows of the fork, he smashed them, and the twelve hens scuttled wildly out and stumbled away over the ruined lawns into the darkness.

Fanned now by the wind that blew in through the shattered windows, the flames leapt higher within the drawing room, until the inner door caught fire. From the wall the blazing portrait of Mrs Spring-Russell in her blue ballgown fell crashing to the floor.

Ape, crossing the hall, saw the burning drawing-room door and heard the crackle of the flames. His immediate thoughts were to save his animals and his house, in that order. The creatures in the music room were most at risk, he knew, because if the fire got into the hall, they might be cut off.

Hurriedly he opened a cupboard where coats and hats and walking-sticks were kept – and also, he knew, an old suitcase.

In the music room he caught the spotty doe rabbit and the two guinea-pigs and thrust them into the suitcase. Then he managed to grab the canary from its golf-club swing.

Holding the bird in one large hand and the case in the other, he went back into the hall, only to find that the fire had burst out of the drawing room and that now a wall of flames barred his way to the kitchen. And in the kitchen were shut Speedy and Uncle Bob!

Somehow Ape made his way back to the front door, his only way out now, and stumbled down the steps. So relieved was he to see two figures approaching, Jake with Speedy on a lead and Joe carrying the parrot in his cage, that it took him a moment to remember that, though the animals were rescued, he'd done nothing yet to save the house.

'The fire brigade!' he said. 'We must telephone the fire brigade!'

'Jake's done it, Mr Ape,' said Joe. 'He dialled 999 while I was getting the animals out.'

'Good boy!' said Ape.

'We were only just out of the kitchen in time,' said Joe. 'It'll be well alight by now. As the whole house will be before long, I'm afraid.'

Which, by the time the fire brigade arrived, it was.

The firemen did their best, running hoses up from the stable-yard and playing them upon the inferno, but they fought a losing battle. Penny Royal, given to Ape's ancestor by Charles II, burned to the ground on the very day on which, nearly 400 years earlier, Guy Fawkes had tried to kill King Charles's grandfather, James I.

Meanwhile, by the light of the flames Joe and Jake had managed to find all the dazed hens that were squatting around in shrubberies and flower-beds, and had put them in the kitchen garden with Columbine and Hollyhock. There they would at least be safe for the night – no fox could climb those walls – and in there, too, were put the rabbit and the guinea-pigs.

As for the canary, Joe offered to take it back to the caravan. 'I've still got my father's old canary-cage,' he said.

'All right,' said Ape wearily.

'Now, Mr Ape,' said Joe. 'You must get some rest. Where will you sleep tonight?'

'Sleep?' said Ape. 'I don't know.' He shook his head. 'I don't know,' he said again.

'Mr Ape,' said Jake, 'you could sleep in the Rolls-Royce. On the back seat. It'd be very comfy. There's that big car-rug to keep you warm.'

Ape managed a smile. 'Jake,' he said, 'I don't know what I'd do without you.'

'Good boy, Jake,' said Uncle Bob.

Much later, long after the gypsies had gone, the fire officer came to Ape. 'I'm sorry, Mr Spring-Russell,' he said. 'There wasn't much we could do – the fire had taken too strong a hold by the time we got here. Any idea what started it?'

Ape shook his head. 'We had a bonfire,' he said, 'and some fireworks.'

The fireman nodded. 'November the fifth,' he said with a sigh. 'Not one of our favourite nights, I'm afraid. Your family lived here long, sir?'

'Best part of four hundred years,' said Ape.

'You on your own now?'

'Yes.'

'Look on the bright side, sir,' said the fireman. 'Think what you can do with the insurance money. You could build yourself a nice little bungalow here with all the mod. cons. Ah well, there's nothing more we can do tonight. We've damped it all down. We'll be back in the morning to have a look round but, to tell the truth, there's not much left to burn.'

Even when the fire brigade had coiled their hoses and left, Ape still stood before the ruins of the house, his dog at his side, his parrot on his shoulder.

Once the fire had consumed the ground floor, it had raged upwards to the second and third floors and the attics. And the fifteen bedrooms and all the other rooms of the upper part of the house had fallen into the burned-out remains of drawing room and dining room, of music room and sewing room, of flower room and library and billiard room and butler's pantry, and, of course, upon the gutted kitchen and the glowing ashes of Ape's four-poster bed.

All that remained were the outer walls, whose stones the fire could not destroy.

At long last Ape turned and shambled away, his long arms hanging low, while behind him, in the coming light of dawn, wisps of smoke still eddied from the gaping blackened window-holes of the great house called Penny Royal.

Chapter 11

Ape Buys a House

When Ape woke next morning, he could not think, for a moment, where on earth he was. Instead of the canopy of the big four-poster bed, he was looking up at a low roof not far above his head, the roof, it seemed, of some building.

Then he realized that he was lying, his knees drawn right up, across the back seat of the old Rolls-Royce, the Silver Ghost, in the coach-house of the stable block.

Throwing off the car-rug that covered him, he struggled to sit up and stretch out his cramped legs. From the front he heard the slap of a tail upon the seat cushions and then Speedy's narrow head appeared over the top of the passenger seat. On top of the steering-wheel perched Uncle Bob.

Sometimes, by sheer luck, the parrot said the correct thing, as now, when he wished Ape a good morning.

'Good morning, Uncle Bob,' replied Ape, but to himself he said that it was a terrible morning. His home, which had been the home of his family for so long, was no more. The great house was gone. Wearily, the old man put his head in his hands.

Joe saw him sitting thus when he entered the coach-house, the lurcher Swift at his heels. Poor old fellow, he thought, what's to become of him? Quietly he went out again and, taking up an empty bucket, let it fall upon the cobbles with a loud clang.

In a few moments Ape appeared, yawning and stretching.

'Good morning, Mr Ape,' said the gypsy. 'You could do with some breakfast, I expect?'

'Not hungry,' said Ape.

'Look,' said Joe. 'Why not drive into town and to a café and have a good fry-up? Leave Speedy here with Swift if you like, and the parrot, if you think he'll stay with me.'

'I am extremely busy,' said Uncle Bob.

'I'll put him in the kitchen garden till you get back, Mr Ape,' said Joe. 'He can't get out of there and he can have a nice chat with the hens.'

'Silly old chap,' said the parrot.

As Ape drove the Rolls out of the coach-house, something felt wrong to him. He glanced at himself in the rear-view mirror and saw what it was. He had no hat. His old brown bowler had, of course, been burned to grey ashes in the hall cupboard, along with all the other hats and coats and walking-sticks.

Then it occurred to him that all his clothes had gone. He owned none except what he now wore – his hairy tweed suit, one shirt, his old school tie, his brown boots.

'One thing's certain,' he said as he drove up to the common. 'I must buy myself some sort of camp bed. I can't sleep another night in this car – I'm as stiff as a board. Oh dear, what's to become of me?'

But half an hour later, he felt much better. He'd found that he was in fact starving hungry, and he'd had a splendid fry-up – eggs, bacon, sausages, mushrooms and fried bread.

Leaving the café, Ape bought a local newspaper and sat in the Rolls to look at it. His eye was immediately caught by an item in red print at the foot of the front page.

STOP PRESS NEWS
STATELY HOME BURNED TO GROUND

Last night was, literally, Bonfire Night for Penny Royal, home of Mr A. P. E. Spring-Russell. This magnificent house, which has belonged to the Spring-Russell family for almost four centuries, was reduced to a shell by an all-consuming blaze which the local fire brigade was powerless to control. Neither Mr Spring-Russell nor a family of gypsies at present camping on the common, who were the only witnesses, were able to say what caused the fire.

Ape gave a deep sigh. Then he said, 'No use crying over spilt milk,' and opened the paper. By chance he opened it at the advertisement section, at a column headed CARAVANS.

Ape stared at the word unseeingly, his mind still filled with yesterday's drama, his bones still aching from his less than comfortable night's sleep in the car. 'Much as I love you, old girl,' he said to the Silver Ghost, 'you are not the most relaxing place to sleep,' and then he focused properly on that word CARAVANS, and suddenly he knew exactly what he was going to do.

'Golly whiskers!' he cried. 'I'll buy one! I'll buy myself a caravan! Today. Now. This very minute,' and he began to read the column carefully. The biggest local suppliers, it seemed, were Comfihome Caravans.

Ape started the car and drove off.

He parked the Rolls on the forecourt of the caravan centre and went in.

A number of different types of caravan were parked in rows, and a smooth-looking young salesman came forward.

Funny-looking old customer, this, he thought as Ape shambled towards him, long arms hanging. He noted the suit, the shirt, the tie, all crumpled and dirty from the smoke and filth of the fire, and the brown boots badly in need of polish. Tramp, is he? he said to himself? Looks as though he's slept in his clothes. Which, of course, Ape had.

Managing to stop himself saying, 'What do you want?' the salesman said instead, 'Can I help you?' It did not occur to him to say 'sir'.

'Yes,' said Ape. 'You can sell me a caravan. I shall want it delivered today, I've no towbar on the old girl,' and he pointed to the Silver Ghost and produced a gold credit card from his pocket.

'Yes, sir, yes, sir, certainly, sir,' said the salesman. 'What type had you in mind?'

'Smallest possible,' said Ape. 'It's just for me.'

'Even our smallest range accommodates two, sir,' said the salesman.

'Well actually, we're three altogether,' said Ape. 'Me and my puppy and my parrot. Just show me the smallest one you've got. All I need is a bed, a table, and something to cook on.'

'Oh, it will have all those and much more,' said the salesman. 'Including a chemical toilet.'

'A what?' said Ape. 'Oh yes, I see what you mean.'

So that afternoon a Land Rover from

Comfihome Caravans towed into the stable-yard at Penny Royal a Bijou Roadmaster de Luxe, and that night Ape and Speedy settled happily down in it, Ape in a comfortable sofa-bed, just long enough for him, Speedy on a rug on the floor, while, from the parrot cage hanging above, Uncle Bob's final sleepy words were 'Home, Sweet Home.'

Chapter 12

Ape Makes a Decision

It must have been that little item in the local newspaper that did it:'. . . a family of gypsies at present camping on the common . . . the only witnesses . . .'

Tongues began to wag.

The fire at Penny Royal was a topic of much interest in the town, and the probable cause of it was plain, in the minds of certain spiteful people. Wherever two or three were gathered together, the same comments could be heard:

'What was a family of gypsies doing up there anyway?'

'You can't trust gyppos. Sly lot, they are.'

'Dirty diddicoys.'

'Shouldn't be surprised if they started the fire.'

'Cooking hedgehogs, I dare say. They do, you know.'

'Sooner they're off the common the better.'

It was not long before some people had convinced themselves, and others, that it was indeed the gypsies who had, for dark reasons of their own, deliberately burned down Penny Royal. Soon Joe became aware that the locals were looking at him differently. Before, they had simply disregarded him, giving him a nod at best and never speaking to him, but now there was staring and pointing and the passing of remarks.

Waiting to collect his son from school, the gypsy overheard two mothers talking:

'Weather's got a lot colder,' said one in a loud voice.

'Yes,' said the other. 'You need a nice fire in the house.'

'Not too big a fire,' said the first. 'You don't want to burn the house down.'

'No,' said the second. 'Not like some people.'

Jake had made quite a few friends, but some of the other schoolchildren began to treat him differently. Nobody actually called him a dirty gyppo, because they remembered what had happened to the bully boy. But there was whispering and giggling and talk behind his back. Jake was made to feel unlike the other children, whose clothes were smarter, who had expensive toys to play with and proper houses to live in, and all this began to make him unhappy.

In his caravan Ape was happy, as he was when training his dog Speedy or taking his donkey Hollyhock for a walk, or feeding his rabbit or his guinea-pigs, which now lived in a loose-box. The hens were a bit of a disappointment now, for the shock of the fire had completely put them off laying, and Ape was having to buy his eggs.

But all the time the grim ruins of the house stood in the background, constantly catching his eye and casting a shadow over his other pleasures.

By now Ape had had the Rolls fitted with a towbar, and was having fun pulling the new caravan up and down the drive, and practising reversing. One day when he had towed the caravan, with Speedy and Uncle Bob aboard it, down to the end of the drive, the thought of escape suddenly occurred to him.

'Suppose I just kept on driving,' he said. 'Driving anywhere, any direction, any distance,

towing my nice new home behind me. I'd never have to look at those terrible accusing fire-blackened walls again. I couldn't do it today, of course, there's too much to fix up first – there's the land to be sold, and the stable block – just right for conversion, that would be, make a nice house for someone, though not for me. But what fun it would be to make a completely fresh start, a new life in some other part of the country, and then to be free to move on again whenever I felt like it, as the gypsies do.'

Even as he spoke these last words, he realized that this plan was only pie in the sky. 'But then if I did that, I'd lose my friends Joe and Jake.'

He turned and drove back to the stable block.

One evening in early December Ape was at the calor-gas stove in his caravan, cooking his supper (tinned mushroom soup with cocktail sausages and baked beans in it), when there was a knock at the door.

'Kindly go away!' said Uncle Bob in Ape's voice. 'I am extremely busy!'

'Who is it?' said Ape.

'It's me, Mr Ape – Joe.'

'Come in, Joe, come in!' called Ape. 'Sit down,

do. What's the matter? Nothing wrong with any of the animals, is there?'

'No,' said Joe. 'But there is something wrong.'

'What?' said Ape.

'Persecution, I suppose you could call it,' said Joe, and he told Ape all about the rumours that had circulated after the fire, and about the dislike – hatred indeed – of him and Jake that this talk had inspired among many of the local people.

'Folk cross the road to avoid meeting me now,' he said, 'and Jake's unhappy at school. It's the old story, Mr Ape, that all Romanies know. Every man's hand is against the gypsies. Except yours, sir. You have always been good to us.'

'This is terrible, Joe,' exclaimed Ape. 'That people should spread such lies. Why, you and Jake risked your lives to save the puppy and the parrot. If anyone burned the house down, I did. I should never have built that bonfire so close.'

Speedy whined softly at the sadness in his master's voice, and Uncle Bob, sitting as usual on Ape's shoulder, gently nibbled at the lobe of his ear.

'I've come to tell you that I've made my mind up, Mr Ape,' said Joe. 'I'm sorry, truly sorry, but it's for Jake's sake, now that folk have turned against us so.'

117

'Made up your mind to do what?' said Ape.

'To leave. To move on once more, away from here. To take to the open road.'

Ape thrust out a hand and Joe took it.

'I wish with all my heart,' Joe said, 'that we did not have to part.'

'We don't,' said Ape. 'I'm coming too.'

Chapter 13

Ape Hits the Trail

His mind made up, Ape could hardly wait to go. But of course there was much to be done first.

On one thing Ape was determined. If Joe and Jake were leaving soon, he wasn't going to hang about here by himself to settle up all his affairs. His house might have gone, but his money hadn't. He was still a rich man, and when the fire insurance claim was paid and the land and the stable block sold, he would be that much richer.

So he called upon the services of a lot of other people to do the work for him – his bank manager, his accountant, his investment adviser, his insurance broker, and the best of the local land agents.

119

'You fix everything up for me,' he told them, 'and then get in touch with me when it's all settled.'

'But where will you be?' each asked.

'No idea,' said Ape, 'but I'll keep you posted.'

The other question that needed to be settled was what was to be done about all the animals?

Ape and Joe discussed this between them.

'You'd better keep the canary,' Ape said. 'He's happy with you, and he'll be more comfortable riding along with you nice and slowly. He'd swing about all over the place once I get speed up in the Rolls.'

Joe smiled, thinking that Ape's usual stately rate of progress would be even slower when towing the heavy caravan. 'Very well, Mr Ape,' he said. 'We'll take the bird, and of course we'll have Billy in the shafts, and Columbine and Hollyhock will be tethered behind us.'

'Well, that's you fixed up,' said Ape. 'As for me, I shall take my dog, of course, as you will, and my parrot, but I don't know quite what to do with the spotty rabbit and the two guinea-pigs. Jake could have them for a Christmas present, if you've got room for them.'

Joe thought for a moment, and then he said, 'Pannier-baskets.'

'I don't follow you,' said Ape.

'We've got a pair of panniers – big wicker-work baskets we sling over Columbine's back, one either side. They could travel in those.'

'Wizard!' said Ape. 'That only leaves the hens. I don't want them mucking up my caravan.'

'Well,' said Joe, 'they're still only laying one or two eggs a day between the twelve of them. I should sell them. Someone will get some nice Sunday dinners out of them.'

In fact Ape gave the hens away to the post-man, who kept chickens. He did not tell Joe that he had extracted a promise from the man that they would not be eaten.

Ape and the Harts had decided between them that they would not set out before the end of Jake's term at school. Because this was not until 22 December, they then decided to wait till after Christmas.

Ape bought maps, and he and Joe pored over them.

'We must have a good start on you, Mr Ape,' Joe said, 'because you'll go ten times as fast as we shall. If you follow the same route, then once you catch us up, we can look about for a suitable place to stay. Which direction do you fancy taking? It's all the same to us.'

'West, I think,' said Ape. 'We'll go west out of Gloucestershire and across the river Severn and into the Welsh hills.'

So they fixed on a route as free from traffic as possible, along lanes and byways, and an eventual meeting-place. The gypsies would set out on Boxing Day, and Ape, because it would give them six days' start and because he thought it a suitable date to begin a new life, would leave on New Year's Day.

On Christmas Day Ape gave another party — a caravan-warming party, he called it.

Joe had driven his own caravan down from

the common and up the drive, to park it in the stable-yard beside Ape's, ready for departure the next morning.

Then they all three squeezed into the Bijou Roadmaster de Luxe, and ate a huge tea, including a Christmas cake which Ape had had specially made. On top of it were two caravans, one drawn by a thirty-horsepower car, one by a single horse.

When they had finished their tea, Ape opened a bottle of wine, and he and Joe raised their glasses (and Jake raised his Coke) and they drank a toast.

'Good luck!' said Ape, and 'Good luck!' replied Joe and Jake and Uncle Bob.

Jake looked worried at parting from his friend the next morning. 'You will come, Mr Ape, won't you?' he said anxiously. 'You will follow us?'

'I will, Jake,' said Ape. 'Cross my heart.'

At the top of the drive he stood, Speedy beside him, Uncle Bob on his shoulder, watching and waving as the caravan, drawn by Billy, the two donkeys walking behind, grew smaller and smaller till it vanished from his sight.

'Right,' said Ape. 'Let's have some breakfast. What d'you say to that, Uncle Bob?'

'Wizard!' said the parrot in Ape's voice.

'Kippers and custard,' said Ape. 'That's what I fancy.' This meant, in Ape language, kippers with scrambled egg.

After that, he ate his favourite mess of creamed rice and strawberry jam and crumbled-up digestives.

Later, when he'd fed his animals, Ape decided to go for a walk. He asked Uncle Bob if he would like to come but the parrot told him he was extremely busy, so he set off with his dog.

Jake had tried his best to teach Ape to whistle like he did, but Ape was hopeless at it. Still, he'd come to a sort of agreement with Speedy. He would put the two fingers in his mouth and make a sort of puffing noise, which was all he could manage, and Speedy (if near enough to hear) would come to him.

Ape walked down the long drive and then up on to the common, where the gypsy caravan had stood. Looking back from this viewpoint, he could see the whole estate of Penny Royal laid out below. At that distance it was not possible to distinguish the chaos of the kitchen garden or the wreck of the lawns or the jungle of the shrubberies: even the ruins of the house looked, at this range, romantic.

Ape stood on the common for a long time, looking down, and as he did so, he suddenly realized that he no longer felt guilty about what had happened. Try as he would, he could not make himself believe that generations of past Spring-Russells were turning in their graves at the thought that their descendant was about to desert the family house.

'It's dead and gone,' he said to Speedy, 'like them, and in six days' time, we'll be going, you and I and Uncle Bob. Then you'll see your mum again and I'll see my friends. Come on, let's go home now, back to our nice new caravan. Because that's what it is from now on – our home, no matter where we are. It ought to have a name really, I suppose.'

Those six days seemed to drag by, so eager was Ape to be gone on the trail of the gypsy family, but at last it was the final day of the old year. Only then did it suddenly become clear to Ape that there was only one thing to call his new home, now that his old one was gone in all but name. So he made a last trip to the supermarket and bought a small pot of paint and a brush.

Had there been any people about very early on the morning of New Year's Day, they would have seen an old Rolls-Royce Silver Ghost pull away from the stable block and set slowly off down the drive, towing a large new caravan in which, had they known it, were a lurcher dog and a green parrot – a caravan on whose door was newly painted in small neat lettering:

PENNY ROYAL

At the wheel of the Rolls they would have seen a large, long-armed old man, wearing a hairy tweed suit and his old school tie and brown boots. Above all, perhaps, they would have noted what a huge, happy, excited grin there was upon the face of Archibald Peregrine Edmund Spring-Russell, the man called Ape.

THE END